Three Kings' Day

by Beatriz McConnie Zapater

Illustrated by
Nayda Collazo Llorens

MULTICULTURAL CELEBRATIONS

MODERN CURRICULUM PRESS

Multicultural Celebrations was created under the auspices of

The Children's Museum, Boston.
Leslie Swartz, Director of Teacher Services,
organized and directed this project with
funding from The Hitachi Foundation.

Design: Gary Fujiwara
Photographs: *2*, Robert Fried;
6, 12, Beatriz McConnie Zapater.

MODERN CURRICULUM PRESS, INC.
13900 Prospect Road
Cleveland, Ohio 44136

ISBN 0-8136-2261-1 (soft cover)   0-8136-2262-X (hard cover)

1 2 3 4 5 6 7 8 9 10   95 94 93 92 91

Simon & Schuster   A Paramount Communications Company

Melinda was in a big hurry to get home.

"I promised Mami I would stop and buy green
bananas and *plantains*," she thought to herself, "but
I have to do it quickly today."

Today, even the grey winter skies above the brownstones could not make her glum. It was January 5, the eve of Three Kings' Day! Tonight the Three Kings would visit Melinda's home on their camels.

Melinda hurried so fast that she almost knocked into Mr. Rivera, the grocery store owner, outside his *bodega*.

"What's the big rush?" laughed Mr. Rivera.

2

"I have to get home to have everything ready for the visit of the Three Kings. They are coming to my house tonight, you know. Tío says that if we really, really believe in them, they will come," she answered.

"Yes, well what do you think they will bring you this year? A pencil case? A beautiful barrette for your hair?" he asked.

"Can you keep a secret?" Melinda asked as she carefully counted out the money Mami had given her. "What I want, more than *anything* in the world, is a pair of roller skates—those white ones. You've seen them. All the girls have them. Well . . . almost all the girls."

5

"Well, I certainly hope you get your wish," Mr. Rivera said. "If not, there's always next year. '¡Feliz Día de Reyes!' to your family. Happy Three Kings' Day!"

When Melinda reached her apartment, everyone was busy. Tío, who was visiting them from Puerto Rico, was watching Mami work in the kitchen. She was grating *plantains* for *pasteles*.

"Oh, Mami—Tío—everything smells so good! I'll start the *arroz con dulce*. The dessert is the best part," Melinda said.

"No," said Mami. "Fernando has been waiting for you. Go help him get the grass and water ready to leave under your beds for the camels."

"That is so silly," said Melinda's older brother Andrés, coming into the kitchen. "Camels? Kings? Why do you waste your time?"

"Mami and Tío say that if we really, really believe the kings will come—they will!" Melinda answered. "Fernando and I must be ready."

"Come on Fernando. First we have to find boxes for the camels' grass. Let's look in the closet."

Fernando found a small box that had once held a bracelet. "Much too small for camels," said Melinda. Then he picked up a grocery box. "A little big, but it will do for me," said Melinda. Then she spotted the box from Mami's shoes. "Here's one for you. It's just the right size for camels," she said, and Fernando grinned.

In the living room, Melinda and Fernando arranged tall brown stalks of grass in their boxes. They had collected the grass from a nearby park the day before. Then Melinda broke a small branch off the bottom of the Christmas tree and put some of it in each box.

10

Later, as everyone was about to sit down for dinner, Tío exclaimed, "Listen, Melinda! Fernando! Andrés! Do you hear the music?"

"It's the Three Kings!" shouted Fernando, clapping his hands.

"No, no, Fernando, not yet," Mami laughed, winking at Tío. "It is a *parranda*. Hear the singing and the guitars?"

The music became louder and louder. "They're right outside our door," she said. "Tío—go invite them in to share our meal. *¡Vamos a reyar!* Let's celebrate!" Soon they were all laughing and singing and eating around the table—even Andrés.

12

After the guests had left, Melinda carried her box of grass and a pan of water to her room. "Tío," she called, "come and see what Fernando and I have ready for the camels."

"This is a meal fit for *any* king's tired camel," Tío said, tucking the blankets around Melinda.

"Are you sure they will come, Tío? Andrés says . . ."

"I am sure, my sweet Melinda. Don't pay any attention to Andrés. This year the Three Kings will come and we will be blessed. Now let's push the box under the bed. It's time for you and Fernando to go to sleep."

15

Melinda closed her eyes. She could hear Tío and Andrés talking in the kitchen. Fernando was breathing softly. She could hear Mami singing a song as dishes rattled in the sink. Then Melinda thought she heard some other noises.

"Those are happy sounds," she thought as she drifted off to sleep. "It sounds like bells . . . footsteps . . . ohhh . . . something is tickling my nose . . . " She pulled the covers up over her head and settled into a dream.

When Melinda opened her eyes again, the dream was gone and sunshine poured through the window. She jumped up and peered under her bed.

"Oh, no, Fernando!" cried Melinda. "The grass is scattered all over the floor, but the box is still here. The Three Kings didn't come. Andrés was right . . . "

Fernando peeked out from his quilt. Slowly Melinda pulled the box out from under her bed. But wait—this box was bigger and was tied with string.

"Oh thank you, Three Kings! I'll never, *ever* doubt you again!" Melinda said as she opened the box. The skates she found inside were the brightest white she had ever seen—and they were exactly her size.

"You know," she said to Fernando who was jumping out of bed. "I know just who I want to show these skates to first. O-h-h-h, Andr-é-s . . . " she called as she hurried out of her room.

Glossary

arroz con dulce (ahr-ROS KOHN DOOL-seh) a dish made of sweet rice and coconut

bodega (boh-DEH-gah) a small grocery store

¡Feliz Día de Reyes! (feh-LEES DEE-ah DEH RAY-yes) Happy Three Kings' Day!

Mami (MA-mee) informal name for mother; mommy

parranda (pah-RAN-dah) a group of musicians and singers that often play special holiday music

pasteles (pahs-TEL-es) plantain dough stuffed with meat, wrapped in a plantain leaf and boiled

plantains (plan-TAYNS) South American fruit resembling green bananas

Tío (TEE-oh) uncle

¡Vamos a reyar! (VAH-mohs AH ray-AHR) Let's celebrate!

About the Author

Beatriz McConnie Zapater grew up in Ponce, Puerto Rico, in a large, close-knit family. She moved to Boston to attend school. The focus of her life is the Puerto Rican community and her two sons, Fernando and Andrés. She dreams of being a musician and a photographer.

About the Illustrator

Nayda Collazo Llorens was born in San Juan, Puerto Rico. She received her Bachelor's Degree from the Massachusetts College of Art in Boston, and is currently living in Santurce, Puerto Rico, working as a graphic designer, printmaker, painter, and illustrator. Through her art, which has been exhibited in Puerto Rico and Massachusetts, Ms. Llorens makes social and political commentaries about the island of Puerto Rico and its people.